You'll Find Me

For Eliza and her daddy,
whose love gave me the words—ARH

To my two babies, Max Wu Yen and Mattiece,
you'll always find me—JL-V

Books for Kids From the
American Psychological Association

Text copyright © 2020 by Amanda Rawson Hill. Illustrations copyright © 2020 by Joanne
Lew-Vriethoff. Published in 2020 by Magination Press, an imprint of the American Psychological
Association. All rights reserved. Except as permitted under the United States Copyright Act of
1976, no part of this publication may be reproduced or distributed in any form or by any means,
or stored in a database or retrieval system, without the prior written permission of the publisher.

Magination Press is a registered trademark of the American Psychological Association.
Order books at maginationpress.org, or call 1-800-374-2721.

Book design by Sandra Kimbell
Printed by Phoenix Color, Hagerstown, MD

Library of Congress Cataloging-in-Publication Data
Names: Hill, Amanda Rawson, author. | Lew-Vriethoff, Joanne, illustrator.
Title: You'll find me / by Amanda Rawson Hill ;
illustrated by Joanne Lew-Vriethoff.
Other titles: You will find me
Description: Washington, D.C. : Magination Press, 2020. | Audience:
Ages 4-8. | Summary: Illustrations and easy-to-read text highlight ways to
find reminders of loved ones in everyday actions, even after they are gone.
Identifiers: LCCN 2019055233 | ISBN 9781433831263 (hardcover)
Subjects: CYAC: Love--Fiction. | Separation (Psychology)—Fiction. |
Parent and child—Fiction.
Classification: LCC PZ7.1.H559 You 2020 | DDC [E]—dc23
LC record available at https://lccn.loc.gov/2019055233

You'll Find Me

by Amanda Rawson Hill • Illustrated by Joanne Lew-Vriethoff

Magination Press • Washington D.C. • American Psychological Association

My dear one.

Life, like spring,
is far too short.

I will not always be…greeting the morning with you.
But you'll find me…in the soft sounds of
slippered feet,
the smell of breakfast tickling your nose,
the way the sun spills into your window,
whispering, *Get up sleepyhead!*

I will not always be…
holding you tight on my lap on our
favorite chair.

But you'll find
me...in the curve
of the cushion,

the first notes of a familiar song,

the satisfaction of finishing a really good book,

something being sipped and savored.

Even though you won't always
see me waving from the crowd,
you'll find me in other ways.

The deep breaths at the beginning,
the burst of speed at the finish.

I'll be in every cheer and *You can do it!*
Even when they're said by lips that aren't mine.

Every hug that warms you

or lifts you off your feet,

every loving glance from eyes that truly see,

a listening ear that hears when you're in need,
they all will hold a part of me.

I will not always be…

around the table for dinners and holidays.

But you'll find me...in the flicker of candlelight,
the pause between *Please* and *Thank you,*

the feel of sprinkles in your palm,
the tinkling of silverware and laughter.

I will not always be…
tucking you in and saying *Good night.*

But you'll find me…
in the touch of covers under your chin,
a wish, a story, a lullaby,
a sliver of moonlight falling across your face,
that space between waking and dreaming.

If you learn to watch with your heart,
you'll find me all around. In the sigh of spring,

a gentle, hair-ruffling breeze.

the soothing shade of your favorite tree.

My love will always be.

And as long as you look with
more than just your eyes…

you'll find me.

Amanda Rawson Hill co-runs a newsletter called *Middle Grade at Heart,* which is a book club kit with a new middle-grade book each month. Her debut middle-grade book was published in Fall 2018. She lives in Atwater, California.
Visit her at amandarawsonhill.com
🐦 @amandarhill32
📷 @amandahillauthor

Joanne Lew-Vriethoff is an award-winning illustrator who received her BA in Illustration from Art Center College of Design in Pasadena, California. She illustrates for picture books, middle grade novels, early readers, and educational books. She lives in Amsterdam.
Visit her at joannelewvriethoff.com
📘 @joannelewvriethoffillustrator
🐦 @jlewvriethoff
📷 @joannelewvriethoff

Magination Press is the children's book imprint of the American Psychological Association. Through APA's publications, the association shares with the world mental health expertise and psychological knowledge. Magination Press books reach young readers and their parents and caregivers to make navigating life's challenges a little easier. It's the combined power of psychology and literature that makes a Magination Press book special.
Visit maginationpress.org
📘 🐦 📷 📌 @maginationpress